hist whist

e.e. cummings

hist whist

illustrated by Deborah Kogan Ray

Crown Publishers, Inc., New York

Published by Crown Publishers, Inc., a Random House company, 225 Park Avenue South, New York, New York 10003
CROWN is a trademark of Crown Publishers, Inc.

Manufactured in Japan

Library of Congress Cataloging-in-Publication Data
cummings, e.e. (Edward Estlin), 1894–1962. Hist whist/
e.e. cummings; illustrated by Deborah Kogan Ray. Summary:
Presents with illustrations the celebrated author's poem of ghosts and goblins, witches, and the devil. 1. Children's poetry, American. [1. American poetry.] 1. Ray, Deborah Kogan, ill. II. Title. PS3505.U334H57   1989   811'.52-dc19   89-596

ISBN 0-517-57360-1
     0-517-57258-3 (lib. bdg.)

10 9 8 7 6 5 4 3 2

hist   whist
little ghostthings
tip-toe
twinkle-toe

little twitchy
witches and tingling
goblins
hob-a-nob   hob-a-nob

little hoppy happy
toad in tweeds
tweeds
little itchy mousies

with scuttling
eyes   rustle and run   and
hidehidehide
whisk

whisk   look out for the old woman
with the wart on her nose
what she'll do to yer
nobody knows

for she knows the devil   ooch
the devil   ouch
the devil
ach   the great

green
dancing
devil
devil

wheeEEE

hist   whist
little ghostthings
tip-toe
twinkle-toe

little twitchy
witches and tingling
goblins
hob-a-nob   hob-a-nob

little hoppy happy
toad in tweeds
tweeds
little itchy mousies

with scuttling
eyes   rustle and run   and
hidehidehide
whisk

whisk   look out for the old woman
with the wart on her nose
what she'll do to yer
nobody knows

for she knows the devil   ooch
the devil   ouch
the devil
ach   the great

green
dancing
devil
devil

devil
devil

wheeEEE